THOMAS & FRIENDS™

Thomas Helps Hiro

Based on
The Railway Series
by the
Rev. W. Awdry

Illustrations by
Robin Davies

EGMONT

EGMONT

We bring stories to life

First published in Great Britain in 2017
by Egmont UK Limited
The Yellow Building, 1 Nicholas Road, London W11 4AN

Thomas the Tank Engine & Friends™

CREATED BY BRITT ALLCROFT

Based on the Railway Series by the Reverend W Awdry
© 2017 Gullane (Thomas) LLC. Thomas the Tank Engine & Friends and
Thomas & Friends are trademarks of Gullane (Thomas) Limited.
Thomas the Tank Engine & Friends and Design is Reg. U.S. Pat. & Tm. Off.
© 2017 HIT Entertainment Limited.

HiT entertainment

ISBN 978 1 4052 8586 5
66574/1
Printed in Italy

Stay safe online. Egmont is not responsible for content hosted by third parties.

Written by Emily Stead. Designed by Claire Yeo.
Series designed by Martin Aggett.

FSC
MIX
Paper
FSC® C018306

Egmont is passionate about helping to preserve the world's remaining ancient forests.
We only use paper from legal and sustainable forest sources.

This book is made from paper certified by the Forest Stewardship Council® (FSC®),
an organisation dedicated to promoting responsible management of forest resources.
For more information on the FSC, please visit www.fsc.org. To learn more about Egmont's
sustainable paper policy, please visit www.egmont.co.uk/ethical

*When Hiro had an accident
that was my fault, I had to help
my friend. I tried to find some
spare parts for him, but ended
up wheel-deep in trouble!
Here's what happened . . .*

One day, Thomas was in the Yard when Hiro pulled up next to him.

"Hello, Hiro! You look shiny! Where are you off to? I'm going to Knapford," Thomas said excitedly.

"Let's go together!" Hiro laughed.

Hiro hurried away, with Thomas racing behind. Thomas had to go very fast to keep up!

Hiro soon slowed for a sharp bend, but Thomas pumped his pistons even faster.

"Watch me go!" Thomas teased, racing ahead.

As Thomas **rocked** around the bend, his cargo came loose, and **rolled** onto the track.

Hiro hit the pipes, and **crashed** to a stop on his side. Thomas felt terrible.

Rocky and Edward were called to help Hiro.
A very cross Fat Controller arrived, too.

Hiro was soon back on track, but when he tried
to set off, his axles **ached** and his gears **groaned**.

"You'll need to go to the Steamworks for repair!"
said The Fat Controller.

That night, Thomas was still feeling sad.

"It's my fault Hiro's broken," he told Percy. "And it's not easy to get the parts he needs."

Thomas remembered the last time Hiro had broken down. He was stuck in the woods for a very long time. Then Thomas had an idea . . .

The next morning, Thomas puffed to where he had first met Hiro, a long time ago.

"If I can find some of Hiro's old parts, then Hiro can be fixed!" thought Thomas.

Branches **snapped** and brambles **scratched**, as Thomas searched bravely for spare parts. But he didn't find any.

Thomas rolled deeper into the dark and spooky woods, his wheels **wobbling**.

Suddenly, a deer jumped across the track, giving Thomas a fright. He screeched to a stop, but the old rails gave way beneath him.

"Silly me!" said Thomas. "It's just a friendly deer."

When Thomas tried to move, his wheels just spun in the mud. He was well and truly **stuck**!

"PEEP! PEEP!" he whistled. "Help!"

Percy was on a nearby Branch Line, but he didn't hear Thomas calling.

"Can anyone hear me?" Thomas cried sadly.

Later, Harold flew by, on patrol. Thomas whistled as loudly as he could. **"PEEP! PEEP!"**

"That looks like steam from an engine," Harold buzzed. "And that sounds like Thomas!"

Harold hurried away to fetch help, but Thomas thought he hadn't seen him.

"No one can hear me!" Thomas cried.

Then suddenly, the rails began to **rumble**. Rocky **bashed** through the brambles, with Percy behind.

"Thomas!" boomed The Fat Controller. "How did you end up here?"

"I was trying to help Hiro, Sir," Thomas sighed.

"Well, let's get you back on track," said The Fat Controller kindly.

Later at the Steamworks, Thomas told Hiro all about his adventure.

"I'm sorry I didn't find any spare parts to fix you," he sighed.

"But Thomas, I **am** fixed!" Hiro smiled. "The Fat Controller already had some parts for me, in case I ever broke down again."

Thomas beamed from **buffer** to **bumper**!

Hiro smiled, too. "So, are you ready?" he said.

"Ready!" Thomas wheeshed.

The two friends set off together. And this time, Thomas remembered to slow down for the bend!

More about Hiro

lamp

nameplate

boiler bands

cab

hand rail

buffer

coupling rod

coupling hook

Hiro's challenge to you

Look back through the pages of this book
and see if you can spot:

house

deer

pipes

mouse

spade

THE THOMAS ENGINE ADVENTURES

 Thomas
 Percy
 Harold
 James
 Cranky
 Spencer

 Gordon
 Flynn
 Toby
 Henry
 Hiro
 Emily

 Thomas and Bertie's Race
 Thomas Goes Crash!
 Kevin
 Diesel
 Troublesome Trucks
 Charlie

 The Thomas Way
 Thomas' New Friend
 Oliver
 Victor
 Thomas' Trusty Wheels
 Thomas Helps Hiro

EGMONT